Favorite Stories from
from
Cowgirl Kate
and Cocoa
Partners

Favorite Stories from Cowgirl Kate and Cocoa
Partners

Written By **Erica Silverman**

Painted By **Betsy Lewin**

sandpiper
Green Light Readers
Houghton Mifflin Harcourt
Boston   New York

To Elina Gardyenko, a wonderful reader and rider —E.S.

With thanks to Patty Peoples Smith for providing the locale —B.L.

First Green Light Readers edition, 2013

www.hmhbooks.com

The display type was hand-lettered by Georgia Deaver.
The text type was set in Filosofia Regular.
The illustrations in this book were done in watercolors
on Strathmore one-ply Bristol paper.

The Library of Congress has cataloged *Cowgirl Kate and Cocoa: Partners* as follows:
Silverman, Erica.
Cowgirl Kate and Cocoa: Partners/written by Erica Silverman, painted by Betsy Lewin.
p. cm.
ISBN: 978-0-15-202125-2 hardcover
ISBN: 978-0-15-206010-7 paperback
Summary: Cocoa the horse herds the cows with Cowgirl Kate, helps her practice
her roping skills, and wishes he could wear boots instead of horseshoes.
[1. Cowgirls—Fiction. 2. Horses—Fiction. 3. Cows—Fiction.]
I. Lewin, Betsy, Ill. II. Title.
PZ7.S58625Co 2006
[E]—dc22 2004027435

ISBN: 978-0-544-02266-9 paper over board
ISBN: 978-0-544-02265-2 paperback

New Shoes

"Cocoa," said Cowgirl Kate,
"this man has come
to give you new horseshoes."

Cocoa glared at the man.

Then he turned and trotted away.

Cowgirl Kate ran after him.

"What's the matter?" she asked.

Cocoa snorted.

"I don't want horseshoes," he said.

"I want cowboy boots."

"But Cocoa," said Cowgirl Kate,

"you are a horse."

Cocoa snorted again.

"I am a cowhorse," he said,

"and I want cowboy boots, just like yours."

"But they won't fit you," she replied.

"Let me try one," he said.

Cowgirl Kate took off a boot.

She held it for Cocoa.

Cocoa lifted one hoof.

He pushed and pushed,

but he could not get his hoof into the boot.

"I'm sorry," said Cowgirl Kate,

"but cowboy boots only fit people."

Cocoa's head drooped.

"People are lucky," he said.

"Lucky?" asked Cowgirl Kate.

She pointed.

"Cocoa, what do you see on the barn?"

"A horseshoe," said Cocoa.

"And what do you see
    on the house?" she asked.
"A horseshoe," he said.
    She led him down the road.
"What do you see on the fence?"
"*Another* horseshoe," he said.

"Cocoa," she asked, "do you know why
people hang horseshoes everywhere?"
"Of course," said Cocoa,
"because nobody wants to wear them."
Cowgirl Kate shook her head.

"No," she said.
"It's because they believe
    horseshoes bring good luck."
"Good luck?" asked Cocoa.
"I want good luck."
    He galloped back to the barn.

He stood still while the man
put on his new shoes.

Then he trotted outside.

"I am lucky!" he cried.

"I have lucky horseshoes!"

He bumped Cowgirl Kate with his head.

"And you are lucky too," he said.

"You are lucky because you have me."

Partners

"Hurry, Cocoa," said Cowgirl Kate.

"We have to check the cows."

"I'm too hot," said Cocoa.

"Check the cows without me."

"We are partners through hot and cold,"
   said Cowgirl Kate,

"and partners do everything together."

   So Cowgirl Kate and Cocoa checked the cows.

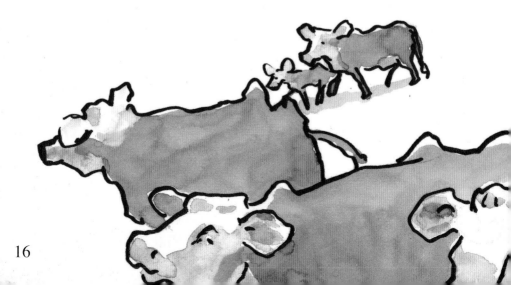

"Those cows sure look hot," said Cocoa.

"They sure do," said Cowgirl Kate.

"Let's move them under the trees."

"I'm too weak," said Cocoa.

"Move them under the trees without me."

"We are partners through weak and strong,"
   said Cowgirl Kate,

"and partners do everything together."

So Cowgirl Kate and Cocoa nudged the cows.
They pushed and prodded until one cow moved,
and another followed, and then another.
Finally, all the cows were standing
in the shade of the trees.
"Look!" cried Cocoa.
"There goes Molly's calf."

Cowgirl Kate and Cocoa
chased him around and around.
When they ran to the right,
the calf ran to the left.

When they ran to the left,
the calf ran to the right.

MOOO!" Molly bellowed. "MOOO!"
The calf stood still.
His ears perked up.
His tail twitched.
"Look!" cried Cocoa.
"He's going back to Molly."
"Good work, partner!" said Cowgirl Kate.

She sighed.

"That calf sure likes to make trouble."

"He sure does," said Cocoa,

"but we are always ready for him."

Cowgirl Kate took her reins.

"We can head back now," she said.

"Not yet," said Cocoa.

"There's one more thing we have to do."

And he trotted . . .

KERSPLASH!

. . . into the river.

"*Ack!*" cried Cowgirl Kate.

"Couldn't you go swimming without me?"

Cocoa turned his head
and splashed water at her.
"We are partners through wet and dry,"
he said,
"and partners do everything together."

Erica Silverman is the author of a series of books about Cowgirl Kate and Cocoa, the original of which received a Theodor Seuss Geisel Honor. She has also written numerous picture books, including the Halloween favorite *Big Pumpkin*, *Don't Fidget a Feather!*, *On the Morn of Mayfest*, and *Liberty's Voice*. Her new easy reader series, Lana's World, will be available from Green Light Readers soon. She lives in Los Angeles, California.

Betsy Lewin is the well-known illustrator of Doreen Cronin's *Duck for President*; *Giggle, Giggle, Quack*; and *Click, Clack, Moo: Cows That Type*, for which she received a Caldecott Honor. She lives in Brooklyn, New York.